New Friends, True Friends,

by Virginia Kroll

Illustrated by Rose Rosely

Stuck-Like-Glue Friends

EERDMANS BOOKS FOR YOUNG READERS

GRAND RAPIDS, MICHIGAN / CAMBRIDGE, U.K.

Text copyright © 1994 Virginia Kroll
Illustrations copyright © 1994 Rose Roseley

Published 1994 by Eerdmans Books for Young Readers,
an imprint of Wm. B. Eerdmans Publishing Co.,
255 Jefferson Ave. S.E., Grand Rapids, Michigan 49503 /
P.O. Box 163, Cambridge CB3 9PU U.K.

Cloth edition 1994
Paperback edition 2000

Printed and bound in Singapore

05 04 03 02 01 00   10 9 8 7 6 5 4 3 2

Library of Congress Cataloging-in-Publication Data

Kroll, Virginia L.
      New friends, true friends, stuck-like-glue-friends / by Virginia Kroll;
      illustrated by Rose Rosely.
            p.   cm.
      Summary: Illustrations and rhyming text provide a look at all kinds of friendships.
      ISBN 0-8028-5085-5 (cloth: alk. paper)
      ISBN 0-8028-5202-5 (pbk: alk. paper)
      [1. Friendship — Fiction. 2. Stories in rhyme.]
      I. Rosely, Rose, 1961–   ill.   II. Title.
      PZ8.3.K8997Ne   1994
      [E] — dc20

Book design by Joy Chu

For Jim Landau, my new friend,
Grace Meyers, my true friend, and
Katherine Smith, my stuck-like-glue friend

V.L.K.

To Hulo Moon and our cosmic family

R.R.

Small friends

Tall friends

Playing-soccerball friends

Talk friends

Chalk friends

Come-and-take-a-walk friends

Wriggly friends
Squiggly friends
Laughing and giggly friends

Riding friends
Gliding friends

Seeking-and-hiding friends

Bumble friends

Humble friends

Toss, turn, and tumble friends

Eating friends

Treating friends

Calling-a-meeting friends

Glad friends

Sad friends

Please-don't-be-mad friends

School friends

Jewel friends

Lounging-by-the-pool friends

Witty friends

Kitty friends

Living-in-the-city friends

Joy friends
Toy friends
Singing girl-and-boy friends

Light friends

Bright friends

Glow-white-at-night friends

Bug friends

Snug friends

Sharing-a-warm-hug friends

Young friends
Old friends
Hot friends
Cold friends

All-kinds-of-weather friends

Always-together friends!